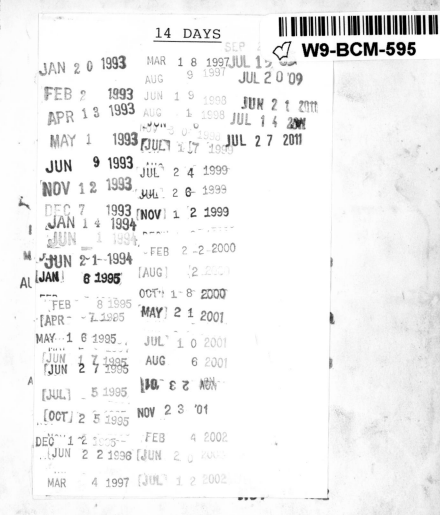

Abig brother can do anything better than you can. He sleeps in a big bed; you're still sleeping in a little bed. He rides a big bicycle and you're still on a little tricycle. Besides, now that your mother's away in the hospital he can really push you around. But wait...

Here come Mother and Father, and they're carrying a brand new baby brother. Now you are a big brother, too!

In a deceptively simple text, Robert Kraus captures the pain of playing second fiddle to an older brother, using pictures of an oversized rabbit as visualized through the eyes of his younger rabbit brother. Then in the last group picture of the rabbit family, we see the relationship as it really is — and that older brother is not *quite so* big, after all!

BIG BROTHER

BY
ROBERT KRAUS

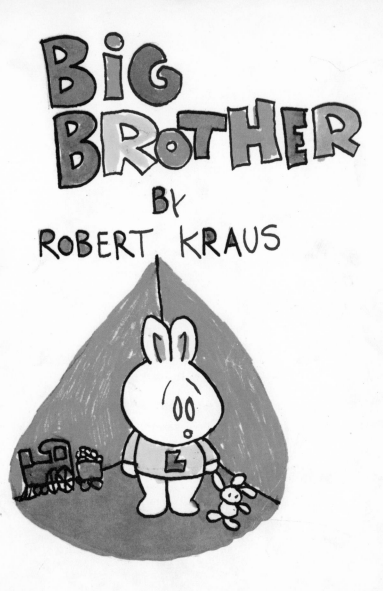

Parents' Magazine Press · New York

Copyright © 1973 by Robert Kraus.
All rights reserved
Printed in the United States of America

Library of Congress Cataloging in Publication Data
Kraus, Robert, 1925—
   Big brother.
   SUMMARY: Troubled by the thought of always being
smaller than his older brother, little brother's worries
diminish when his mother returns home from the hospital.
   [1. Brothers and sisters — Fiction] I. Title.
PZ10.3.K869Bi   [E]   72-8059
ISBN 0-8193-0648-7   ISBN 0-8193-0649-5 (lib. bdg.)

To Pamela, Bruce and Billy

He can do everything

better than I can.

He's got big friends.

I've got little friends.

He's got big clothes and fancy jackets.

I've got little clothes and dinky sweatshirts.

He's got a two-wheeler.

I've got a tricycle.

He's got a great big bed.

I've got a tiny little bed.

I get bigger— but so does he!

The bigger I get, the bigger he gets!

He'll *always* be bigger than I am!

And older.
I can never
catch up!
Never! Never! Never!
I'll always be the little brother.

And—
on top of everything else,
my mother is in
the hospital.

My big brother bosses me around.
"Do this—do that—don't make a mess—

pick up your socks—
    pick up this—
        pick up
            that."

I wish my mother would come home.

She picks up after me.

She's home!

Now *I'm* a big brother too!

The End

A native of Milwaukee, Wisconsin, ROBERT KRAUS moved to New York as a young man to complete his art training at the Art Students League. Initially he found his place as a cartoonist and cover artist for the *New Yorker* magazine, but in 1955 he published his first picture book for children and since then has illustrated, or both written and illustrated, over forty children's books, including *I, Mouse, The Littlest Rabbit, Amanda Remembers,* and *The Bunny's Nutshell Library.* He is the president of Windmill Books which he founded in 1966 and which published the 1970 Caldecott winner, *Sylvester and the Magic Pebble.*

Mr. Kraus now lives in Ridgefield, Connecticut, with his wife and two sons. *Big Brother* is his first book for Parents' and his second, *How Spider Saved Halloween,* will soon be published.